# ALLure

## BY

# Rilwan Salaam

# Dedication

I would like to dedicate this book to All fathers, mothers, children and all heroes in the world. I remember you all...

# About the
# Author

Rilwan Salaam is an MBA graduate with outstanding academic performance from Felician University in New Jersey, United States. He is a dedicated and humble writer with a passion for turning everyday situations into meaningful lessons and stories.

His greatest credentials are dedication, passion, self-discipline. the ability to listen, and a constant drive to improve his craft.

One sunny morning, Lily wandered into the enchanted forest, eager for adventure. Suddenly, she heard a strange, rhythmic croaking that sounded like music.

To her surprise, she saw a bright green frog dancing gracefully on a lily pad, glowing softly in the sunlight.

The frog noticed Lily and paused his dance, bowing politely. "Hello, I am Allure," he said with a cheerful voice, "and I have magical dancing powers."

Lily's eyes widened with wonder as she stepped closer, eager to learn more about her new friend.

Allure explained that his dance could unlock hidden magic in the forest, making flowers bloom and stars twinkle brighter.

Lily was excited and asked if she could learn his dance. With a joyful leap, Allure began to twirl, casting sparkling magic into the air.

As Allure danced, the trees shimmered, and the sky sparkled with tiny glowing lights. Lily clapped happily, feeling the magic fill her heart with joy.

She decided to join in, trying to mimic Allure's graceful moves.

Suddenly, a dark cloud appeared overhead, threatening to block the sunlight and dim the magic. Allure looked worried, but then remembered his special dance could bring back the light.

He danced faster and more beautifully than ever, casting a radiant glow that pushed away the cloud.

The forest brightened again, and the flowers bloomed in vibrant colors. Lily cheered, realizing that her new friend's dance had saved their magical home.

Allure winked and said, "Magic is strongest when friends dance together."

As the day gradually turned to evening, Allure told Lily that his magic could help her find her way home. He performed a special dance that created a glowing path through the trees.

Lily followed the shimmering trail, feeling grateful for her enchanted adventure.

Before she left, Lily hugged Allure and promised to visit him again, soon. Allure croaked happily, promising to always dance and keep the magic alive.

With a wave goodbye, Lily stepped onto the glowing trail, heading back home with a heart full of wonder.

That night, Lily dreamed of dancing frogs and magical forests, feeling happy and inspired. She knew she had found a special friend in Allure and that their magic would stay with her forever.

The enchanted forest was now her secret place of joy and adventure.

# COLORING ACTIVITIES